The Knight of the Cart

The Knight of the
Cart

retold by CONSTANCE HIEATT

illustrated by JOHN GRETZER

Thomas Y. Crowell Company   ·   New York

Retold by Constance Hieatt

SIR GAWAIN AND THE GREEN KNIGHT

THE KNIGHT OF THE LION

THE KNIGHT OF THE CART

Designed by LARRY ALEXANDER

Manufactured in the United States of America

L.C. Card 70-78263

1   2   3   4   5   6   7   8   9   10

For Rachel

Contents

Preface

Of all the names associated with the stories of King Arthur and his knights, that of Sir Lancelot is probably the most familiar to a modern audience. It was not always so. The earliest audiences of these tales were far more familiar with Sir Gawain, for one. But in twelfth-century France, one of the very greatest of the poets who wrote of Arthur's court, Chrétien de Troyes, wrote a romance which tells how Sir Lancelot suffered the humiliation of being the "knight of the cart" in order to rescue Queen Guinevere.

Chrétien tells us that he wrote the story at the request of a great lady of his day, Marie, Countess of Champagne. For many years Lancelot must have been a particular favorite of the ladies, who were a very important part of the medieval audience; Geoffrey Chaucer, for example, assures us in the *Canterbury Tales* that his comic tale of Chanticleer is "just as true as the Book of Lancelot de Lake, that women hold in great reverence." By the time Sir Thomas Malory wrote his *Morte d'Arthur* all sources seemed agreed in calling Lancelot the greatest of Arthur's knights.

Like most other modern writers concerned with the tales of King Arthur—that is, the cycle of stories known to scholars as the "Matter of Britain"—I have drawn on Malory's version; but I have drawn as much or more directly from Chrétien, and, to an extent which might shock admirers of both those great writers, on my own imagination. Many more influences have, of course, left their traces. Those who enjoy hunting sources and explicating allegory could probably find material here, but they are not the audience for whom my tale is intended.

I. Guinevere Lost

*W*hen May *brings blossoms and new green leaves, the* world rejoices that the earth — which seemed dead and withered by winter — has come alive again. Every year the buds of spring bring men new hope and courage, just as they did when the world was young, in the long-ago days of King Arthur.

Thus it came about one year, when spring came to Camelot, that Queen Guinevere wished to go out in the woods and fields to gather up May flowers. "Sire," she said to her husband, the king, "tomorrow is the first of May. Let us give due honor to the season, and ride out to bring in the May."

"Gladly would I join you in this," the king replied with a sigh; "but I fear that I cannot go. I have called a council tomorrow morning, and must then meet with some of our trusted knights, to discuss certain matters of weight. You will miss the best part of the morning, my queen, if you wait until we can join you. But take with you some of the younger knights, to bear you company, and we shall all feast together when you return, and rejoice at the harvest you bring."

So Guinevere chose ten young knights and ten of the fairest ladies, and told them to prepare their freshest attire — green, in honor of spring — and make ready to ride by her side in the morning. Long before daybreak they arose, and as the dawn came they were gathered around their queen, eager to be out and away.

King Arthur stood there to see them off, with his chief knights by his side. Gawain and Lancelot stood on one side, Sir Kay on the other, and many other noble knights were in King Arthur's company. "Do not linger too long," they cried. "Our May Day feast will be waiting!"

The merry group rode off, wandering through many a blooming meadow and into the fragrant woods. When they had gathered so many flowers and leaves that all were decked with garlands and laden with so many boughs that no one could carry more, they turned to ride back to the court. But as they rode through a forest glade, suddenly they found that their path was blocked — and in fact they were quite surrounded by a troop of knights in armor, mounted on huge steeds.

Guinevere's young knights quickly drew their swords and formed a circle around the ladies. But they saw that they could not protect them long, for they were hopelessly outnumbered. Of course, they were ill prepared to fight, for they had come out in their gayest robes, not in heavy armor; there were no steel helmets under the garlands on their heads.

The knight at the head of the grim-looking band rode forward a pace, and addressed the queen. "Lady," he said, "you see well that your men have no chance against me. None of them can hope to live if they are so rash as to fight. If you value their lives, tell them to put down the swords. Whether they live or die, they can in no way help you, for you are my prisoner. You must come away with me; you will never see your lord, King Arthur, again."

"Traitor knight," said Guinevere, "you bring great shame on yourself by this foul deed. Only a craven coward would lie in wait as you have done, rather than challenge my knights to fair combat. You would not have dared try to capture me if Lancelot or Gawain were by my side! Whoever you are, you dishonor only yourself."

"Say what you will," the strange knight said, "you cannot save yourself — or the honor of Arthur's famous court. Know that I am called Malagant, son of King Bademagus, as great a king as any. Yet your lord, in his foolish pride, has never invited me to join his fellowship called the Round Table. Now I shall have my revenge: we shall see how proud the knights of that Round Table are when I have taken their queen from them! I have waited long years for just such a chance to find you thus unguarded; now you have fallen into my hands, and I am heartily glad."

"Nay, sir," cried one of Guinevere's knights; "our lady is not unguarded! Though you are a hundred and we only ten, we shall never let you take the queen while we have life in our bodies." Flashing their swords — their only weapons — the ten

4

young men struck at the spears of their attackers. They held off wave after wave of the foes, fighting with the utmost valor as long as they possibly could. But such an unequal combat could not last long, and, though they fought most valiantly, soon all ten of the queen's defenders were sorely wounded. Some lay as if dead on the ground, others swayed in their saddles, exhausted.

The queen, fearing that they would all be slain, cried out in sorrow: "Sir Malagant, do not slay my noble knights! I will go with you, as you ask, if you will attend to their wounds, and see that they are hurt no more. But they must come with me; unless they may bear me company, I will never go with you. I would sooner kill myself."

"Madame," answered Malagant, "for your sake they shall be spared — providing you will ride with me and obey my commands. But all must come together, under guard, to my castle in the land of Gorre, where none can make trouble for me."

Guinevere knew well why Malagant wished to keep them all together. If anyone there got away alive, and returned to Arthur's court, it would not be long before he and his knights heard of the queen's capture and rode out to rescue her. Secretly, she called aside a young page, who was devoted to her service. She told him, "As soon as you see a chance, slip away and ride quickly back for help. Take this ring to Sir Lancelot. He will know that it means I need his help as never before. Ride swiftly, for my sake!"

So the page watched for a moment when no one was looking his way. When he saw his chance, he spurred his horse, whirled around, and was gone in an instant. As soon as Sir Malagant realized what had happened, he sent some of his best knights riding after the page; but they could not catch up with him, and he escaped clean away.

"Madame," said Sir Malagant, "you have done this to betray me, for you hope to be rescued. But I tell you that your hope is vain. No one, not even Sir Lancelot, will find it easy to come to your aid."

6

Grimly, he ordered the troop to make haste, so that they might lock the queen in his distant castle before anyone could catch up with them. But first he ordered thirty archers to lie in wait for pursuers, saying, "If any knight from Arthur's court should try to follow us, use your bows and arrows to keep him from getting any further, unless it be a knight on a white horse. That would be Sir Lancelot, and it is dangerous to fight him, no matter how many of you there are. If he should come this way, see that you slay his horse; that will be enough to stop him. But do not attack the knight himself, for few who have done that have lived to tell the tale."

Now the rest of the band rode on, closely guarding the queen and her ladies, and escorting the wounded knights, who made a most pitiable sight: few of them could sit upright on their steeds. They passed over plains and through great forests, through towns and over rivers, hardly stopping to rest, until at last they came to an immense castle on an island in the sea. There they were to be imprisoned.

The queen's heart sank when she saw that stronghold. Surely no knight could hope to enter there against the will of the lord of that land. The boatman who ferried them out through the choppy waters obeyed his lord, and would never carry a stranger. Nor was there a bridge to the land, except for a narrow shaft of glittering steel, with edges ground as sharp as any sword, which spanned the water on one side of the island; on the other, there was a bridge indeed — but so far under the water that no man could cross it in safety.

So Guinevere passed over the deep water into the dark halls of the castle, far from the blossoming fields of Camelot.

2. The Knight in the Cart

*A*round *the Round Table at Camelot, Arthur and his best* knights had long been sitting in council. They were troubled, for they knew that many good men of the realm had disappeared mysteriously: no one knew what had happened to them. Some said that this had gone on for years, and others had noted it only of late. Recently, they had heard some strange stories. Travelers said that there was a land where many of Arthur's subjects now dwelt in captivity, never to return. This land was said to be in the north, or so some said; others were sure it was far in the west, and there were those who argued that it was east — or south.

But no one had proved that there was such a land, and, in the end, the Round Table decided that there was nothing as yet they could do. They did not even know if there was an enemy, much less what enemy it might be. Some, who had lost dear friends, grumbled that Arthur's realm was not what it used to be, if this sort of thing could go on — but even they had no idea what could be done. And so the council came to an end. Some went back to their lodgings, to think over the tidings they had just heard; others stretched and sniffed, wondering if it were not time to dine.

Now, as it drew near the dinner hour, Sir Gawain suddenly realized that the queen had still not returned from her Maying. She had promised to be back by the middle of the morning, but noon had passed and she was not yet there. Turning to his uncle the king, he said, "My lord, I wonder much that my lady the queen is so long away. If you will give me your leave, I will gladly ride out and seek for her."

"Good nephew," said Arthur, "you speak as a courteous knight. Indeed, you are right, and I will ride with you myself. Pray God that my lady has met no misfortune!"

But while they were preparing to go, the queen's page rode into Camelot, galloping straight to Sir Lancelot's lodging. When Lancelot saw Guinevere's ring in her messenger's hand, and heard how she had been carried away, he jumped to his feet with a cry of anguish: "Alas, my queen!" he said; "I would give all the gold in the world to have been by your side this day! Alas, my dear lord King Arthur — the glory of your kingdom is this day departed, if we cannot even keep our queen from the hands of the enemy! But this I solemnly vow: never again shall I see the fair halls of Camelot until I have returned their brightest treasure, our lady Queen Guinevere. May I die in disgrace if I cannot defeat the traitor who has dishonored us all!"

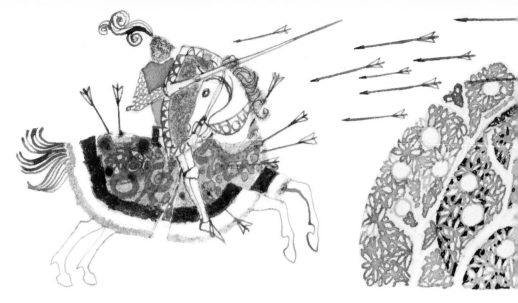

He called at once for his weapons, and, losing no time, armed himself in all haste. As he mounted his great white horse, he turned back to the page and said, "Go now to Sir Gawain, and tell him your tidings. Bid him ride after me. If he would join me, he should not stop until he finds where Malagant has carried the queen — for wherever she is, there he shall find me too. If I live, I shall rescue her, and take vengeance on the wretch who defies us all."

As Lancelot rode away, the page went to look for Sir Gawain. He found him with the king, and many other noble knights, preparing to go out after the queen. When they had heard his tidings, they did not linger to grieve: every man took to his horse, and all rode off as fast as they could — some in one direction, some in another, all in search of Queen Guinevere.

Lancelot, meanwhile, rode far ahead. He came into the wood where Malagant's men had earlier trapped the queen, and there at that same spot the thirty archers barred his way, bidding him to turn back. "What!" cried Lancelot. "Do you think you can keep me from my way? I have no fear of such cowards as you, hiding behind your ditches and hedges: if there were

four times as many there, you would never dare to stop me!"

"Yet you shall halt, sir knight," said an archer, "or go your way on foot; for if you persist, your horse shall surely be slain."

And, as Lancelot still defied them, they shot his white horse with many arrows, so that the knight had to dismount. But, before he could reach them behind their many defenses, they turned their own horses and fled, so that he could not catch up with them.

"Oh, shameful," said Sir Lancelot, "that ever one knight should deal so with another! It is truly said that a good man is in greatest danger when his foe is a coward."

Then there was nothing he could do but walk, and he walked on for a while, sorely weighed down by his armor, his shield, and his heavy spear. It was weary, hot work for a warm spring day, but he would not put down any of his arms, for fear of Sir Malagant's treachery.

About this time, Gawain rode into that same wood, and saw there in the clearing a great white horse lying on the ground, wounded with many arrows. He found this a grievous sight. He suspected that this must be Lancelot's horse, but he saw no sign

13

of Sir Lancelot. So he rode on through the wood until he came to a rough roadway. As he looked down along this road, he saw, some way ahead of him, a knight, fully armed, going along on foot. Just as Gawain realized that this knight was Lancelot himself, he saw that the knight had overtaken a cart, which was hauling wood from the forest. A mean-looking dwarf was riding in the cart. Gawain heard Lancelot hail the dwarf, asking him whether the queen had passed this way.

The dwarf did not seem to hear. He rode on, scowling ferociously, looking neither to left nor to right. But Lancelot ran alongside the cart, grasping the horse's bridle in his hand, imploring the dwarf to answer him. When the dwarf could no longer ignore him — for indeed, the cart horse had slowed to a halt — he finally said in a surly tone, "Get into the cart."

"Friend," said Lancelot patiently, "I ask you nothing but this: Have you seen a fair lady pass this way, guarded by a company of knights?"

But the dwarf would by no means answer him. All he would say in reply was, "If you wish to see the queen again, get into my cart; I will take you where you shall hear tidings."

Now, as it happened, in those days no good knight would willingly ride in a cart. When a man was convicted of a great crime, he was placed on just such a cart, and dragged through the streets of the towns to be held up to shame and ridicule. Therefore if a knight were seen in a cart, the people would hold him disgraced, and he would never be welcome again in any decent man's hall. Gawain knew this well. He was, then, horrified when he saw Sir Lancelot jump into the cart and ride along like a common criminal.

14

Lancelot dreaded dishonor as deeply as anyone could. But there was no other way. If the queen were not rescued, he and all of Arthur's court would be dishonored forever. To save the queen, he would have to endure the disgrace. And so he rode with the ugly dwarf, urging him to make greater speed. Gawain, shocked as he was by this sight, spurred his horse and followed the cart.

And trotting after Sir Gawain, there followed Sir Lancelot's horse — a strange sight indeed, with more than forty arrows in his sides!

15

3. The Damsel of the Tower

*T*hus this odd company rode along: first a cart, in which there rode a tall knight and a dwarf; then a knight on horseback, following the cart; and a great white horse with no rider, bristling with arrows, trailing along behind.

Late in the afternoon they came to a town on the side of a hill, and went up the road through the gate. When the towns-people saw a knight in a cart, they thought he must be a criminal. They shouted insults and jeered at him. "Is this a robber, dwarf?" they cried. "Or is it a murderer brought to be hanged?"

But the dwarf made them no reply, though the people now began to throw mud as well as insults. He drove on silently, up the long, steep hill, to a great tower high above the town. There a fair damsel came out to greet them, attended by two gentle maidens. She greeted Gawain courteously, before she turned to the dwarf and asked, "But who is the criminal in the cart? Why is he brought here thus?"

Again the dwarf said nothing at all. Gawain stepped forward and said, "This is no criminal, dear lady, but as good a knight as lives in this world."

"Then why," she asked, "does he ride in a cart?"

"That is his misfortune," said Gawain.

"It is a misfortune indeed," said the lady politely. But her tone was cold, and so was her face when she glanced at Lancelot. Then she saw the sad state of the wounded white horse, and went to see that the arrows were drawn and the wounds properly tended, while her servants helped the two knights disarm and wash before supper.

When they were ready, and dressed in fresh clothing the damsel had sent for their use, they were led to the table and served an excellent meal. The fair damsel sat by Sir Gawain's side, and showed him every honor. When they had eaten their fill, and the wine had been passed around, the two knights were taken to their beds. They slept well until the next morning.

At daybreak Lancelot arose and climbed to the top of the tower, where he could look out over plains and hills over all the country roundabout. Looking in one direction, he saw, not too far away, the wood through which he had come in the cart; beyond it Arthur's land must lie, but that he could not see. His eyes now followed the road which led past the tower, and he saw that it branched into two paths, just before it came to a broad river; and beyond that he saw a land he had never seen before. It was veiled in the morning mist, but he could barely see, far off in the distance, the tower of a castle.

As he leaned on the ledge of the window, trying to see more clearly the land which lay beyond, Gawain and the lady came up, and were alarmed to see him lean out so far. Quickly Gawain put out a hand to draw Sir Lancelot back, saying, "I beg you, sir, be more careful of your life!"

"Perhaps he would be better dead than alive," said the damsel of the tower. "Since he has ridden in a cart, his disgrace will be known far and wide, and he shall suffer shame and sorrow." But she meant them no ill will, and presently she added, "Gentle knights, if you wish to tell me where you are bound, or what your quest may be, perhaps I could be of help to you."

When the two knights had told her how they came to be seeking for their queen, she hesitated a moment before she replied. "If that is your errand," the lady said, "you shall indeed endure much suffering. It is a dangerous journey. Do you see, there beneath this tower, where the road branches two ways? One goes off through the forest, and the other leads to the river. Both ways lead to the land of Gorre, and to the castle at the far end of that land. It is to that castle that Malagant must have taken your queen. That is it in the distance there — you can just see the tower rising out of the mist."

"Lady," said Gawain, "you give us new hope, for surely that castle is less than a day's ride away."

"Nay," said the damsel. "I fear it is not so. Only a native of that land could make the journey in one day. For a stranger, the way is perilous — not least when he reaches his goal. That is the kingdom from which no visitor returns; all who go there must

remain in sorrow and exile. There are many there from your kingdom, sad and worn down with care, for they may never escape."

"Yet perchance we may free them," Gawain replied. "But you say that there are two paths. Pray, gentle damsel, show us which one we should take."

"That I cannot say," said the damsel, "for they are equally terrible. It is not easy to enter that land without the permission of its king — or, rather, of his son, for King Bademagus is old, and Malagant rules the land. The nearer the roads draw to his castle, the more dangerous they are. Yet I will tell you the truth: the castle may be entered by one of two ways. The first is called the water-bridge, for it is under water, with a bottomless sea beneath it. The bridge is less than two feet wide, and is slippery and treacherous. The first road you see before you, that which goes through the forest, leads directly to the water-bridge.

"The second entry may be worse, for it is just like a sharp sword. It is called the sword-bridge, and no man has ever passed that way. The road toward the river leads to the sword-bridge."

The two knights regarded the paths below in silence for a few moments. There seemed little to choose between them, for both were extremely perilous. At last Sir Lancelot said, "Lord Gawain, I think we had better part. If you follow one path and I the other, perhaps one of us may succeed in the end. What say you, which way will you choose?"

"I do not know," said Gawain, "for both seem as bad as could be, and it is hard to say which is worse. But since you ask me to make a choice, I will follow the road to the water-bridge."

"Then I shall go to the sword-bridge," said Sir Lancelot.

"On foot," asked the damsel, "or on a cart? For your horse is not fit to travel."

"Madame," said Lancelot, "since I must, I will go on foot."

"Nay," said the damsel, "that you will not — I see I have teased you enough. You shall have a horse from my stable, and I will care for yours until he is well again. You are both brave knights, and I pray that God shall watch over you. You especially, Knight of the Cart, will be in need of His aid!"

Now she led them back down to her hall, and would not let them depart until they had had food and drink. Then she wished them well, and they parted, each of the two knights to follow his separate path, while the lady remained in her tower, watching from her high window as they rode off on their way.

4. The Land of Gorre

Bidding farewell to Sir Gawain at the fork of the road, Sir Lancelot turned to the right, into the path that led to the sword-bridge, and rode on until he drew near the bank of the river. There he reined in his horse and looked about for a crossing place. There was neither ferry nor bridge, but there was a well-marked ford. On the further bank of the river there was an armed knight, keeping guard over the ford, and by his side was a young damsel, mounted on a palfrey.

Lancelot turned his horse toward the ford, but at that moment the knight on the opposite shore cried out, "Hold, sir knight! I am guarding this ford, and I forbid you to cross."

"Make way," answered Lancelot, "for I shall certainly cross right here."

"That you shall not," cried the knight; "I will cut you down before you set foot on our land. We want no such outcasts here. We have been warned of your coming: you are the knight who rode almost up to our borders like a common criminal. Turn back, Knight of the Cart, or you will surely regret it!"

Lancelot feared no man's threats. Wasting no further words, he simply rode forward into the ford. The knight of the ford, enraged, put his horse into a gallop and bore down with his lance, knocking Lancelot off his steed in the middle of the ford. Lancelot's spear flew from his hand, and his shield slipped from his neck. "Ha!" cried the other knight, as he moved back on his bank of the river. "Such a ducking was what you deserved! You will get nothing but shame for your pains if you try to cross over this ford."

Grieved that he had made such a bad start, Lancelot reached

for his spear and shield, which were drifting down the stream; but they were now so far away that he could not reach them and hold on to his horse at once. Grasping his horse's bridle, he answered, "Sir knight, if you will not give me a courteous welcome, will you at least grant me a fair fight?"

"Gladly," said his opponent. "I shall be happy to teach you a lesson."

"Then let me retrieve my shield and my spear, that we may meet on even terms."

The knight of the ford granted this. When Lancelot had re-armed and mounted his horse, the two knights charged at

each other, meeting right in the middle of the ford. There they exchanged sharp thrusts until both had broken their lances. Finally Lancelot drove the knight of the ford back onto his bank; both had drawn their swords, and the battle continued, half in the water and half on land.

Both were brave and skillful knights, and as they traded blow after blow the battle lasted so long that Lancelot became greatly ashamed. How could it take him so long to deal with a single knight — he, who had defeated ten men at once on many another occasion! Redoubling his efforts, at last he pressed on so hard that the other knight was forced to step back and give him room on the shore.

28

On firm ground, at last Lancelot was able to deal such great strokes with his sword that it was not long before the knight of the ford was at his mercy. By now he was so enraged that he certainly would have dealt a deathblow, but at that moment he heard a cry, as the young damsel, who had been watching the fight, spoke out in fear and grief: "For God's sake, sir," she said, "and for mine — show mercy to my knight! I beg you to let him live, for I swear he shall do you no further harm."

Sir Lancelot replied, "Since you ask it so, maiden, I needs must grant your request." And he put down his sword.

The damsel knelt down before Lancelot, weeping in gratitude; she said, "Good sir, you are truly a courteous knight. You will never regret granting my boon, for I swear that when the time comes, I shall repay you well."

"And for my part," said the defeated knight, "I vow that I shall always be a true friend to you."

And so Sir Lancelot gave them both leave to go wherever they wished, and he turned on his way once more. Leaving the river behind him, he rode through a deserted countryside for the better part of the day, until he came to a fair chapel, set in a pleasant field. Here he dismounted and left his horse to graze while he went in to say his prayers.

When he had finished he rose to go, but as he went out of the chapel he noticed what seemed to be a strange monument in the churchyard there. Resting on a finely carved base was a huge stone tablet, on which a message was engraved, but so high up that he could not read the words. As he stood and gazed at this stone slab, an old man appeared, dressed as a hermit, and greeted him fairly enough. Lancelot returned his greeting, and asked him what that great stone might be.

"It is beautiful, is it not?" said the hermit. "There is still more rich ornament within the base where it stands, but you cannot see that, for seven of the strongest men in the world could not raise that stone. You may see that there are words written above, on the top of the tablet; they say that he who can raise this stone alone will set free the captives in this land, from which no stranger can depart."

At once Sir Lancelot took hold of the stone, and in a moment he had raised it easily. The hermit stood frozen in astonishment — he did not know what to think. Finally he found his voice, and asked, "Who, then, are you, who can lift up a stone that would be too much for seven good men? Are you he who was to come in shame, suffering the scorn of the people, who alone can rescue the prisoners of this land?"

"I am called the Knight of the Cart," Sir Lancelot replied, "but I know no more than you do what my fate in this land is to be. I do indeed seek for a prisoner, who is held, as I am told, in a great castle in this land."

"I commend you to God," said the hermit, and bowed to him in farewell.

5. To the Sword-Bridge

*E*arly that morning, Lancelot came to a place where the road grew narrow between two rocky cliffs. There was hardly room for a man on a horse to ride through this passage, and Lancelot thought it looked like an excellent place for a trap. Before he rode on, he looked about him carefully. Up on the top of one of the cliffs, he saw a wooden tower. This was a guard-house, where there was always a knight on duty, guarding the rocky pass.

An armed knight in the tower had seen Lancelot approach. He was now down in the roadway, backed by two servants carrying axes. "Fool," he said to Sir Lancelot, "a man who has ridden in a cart can never pass this way. Flee, or you shall soon regret the day you boldly entered this land!"

The two knights rode at each other just as hard as they could, and in the moment when they met the other knight's lance shattered on Lancelot's shield. But the force of Lancelot's blow was such that he knocked his foe off his horse. Now the two servants closed in, brandishing their axes. Lancelot swerved quickly out of their way before they could stop their strokes. The blades of both axes struck into the hard ground and were firmly stuck. When the two servants, now weaponless, saw that Lancelot was about to charge straight forward, jumping his horse over the axes embedded in the earth, they quickly got out of his way, rather than be trampled.

Sir Lancelot did not give another glance to either the fallen knight or his servants, but rode swiftly on his way, now that the passage was clear.

He met no one else on the road for some time, until, when

the noonday sun was high above, he saw a charming young damsel coming his way, richly dressed and lovely to look upon. She rode without any attendants, and drew up when she met Sir Lancelot. "Hail, noble knight," said she; "I have long waited for you."

Lancelot returned her greeting courteously, and asked what she would have of him.

"Your love," the maiden replied. "My house is prepared to receive you, and a great feast awaits. Come with me, and you shall know such joy this day that no man could desire more."

"Lady, I thank you," said Lancelot, "for the great honor you would do me. But I have made a solemn vow, and I cannot turn aside from my road."

"Do not reject me, sir," she begged; "although I ride alone today, I am mistress of a great estate — my meanest servants are dressed in silk, and the worst dish in my house is made of solid gold."

As courteously as he could, Lancelot continued to refuse, until at last the maiden said, with a sigh, "But there is one boon you must let me have: allow me to ride a way in your company, for I have left all my servants at home, and am in need of protection."

A courteous knight could not refuse to escort a defenseless lady, and so for a while Lancelot must needs slow his pace a bit, as the maiden rode by his side. Soon they came to a little valley, where a path went off to one side. The lady turned her horse toward this path, saying, "Sir, here is a better way. Follow me, and I shall guide you well."

"You may go as you wish," said Sir Lancelot, "but as for me, I will not leave my road until I have followed it to the end."

"But I assure you solemnly that the other is better," the damsel insisted.

"The path which I follow leads straight ahead, and I shall not turn aside from it. If you wish to ride with me, you will have to come this way."

The damsel turned back reluctantly, and rode in silence by his side as they made their way steadily forward. From time to time she glanced about her, as if she expected to see someone come. Lancelot did not fail to notice this, and watched carefully to see what would happen next.

They came around a bend in the road, and there before them was a meadow, where a group of knights and ladies were engaged in sport. As soon as she caught sight of them, the damsel by Lancelot's side suddenly began to tear her garments and raised her voice in a piercing scream. "Help!" she cried. "Help! Oh, help a poor maiden, led off against her will!"

The knights, who had been dancing and playing games there, ran for their weapons and horses and rushed at Lancelot, shouting, "Here is the villainous Knight of the Cart! Let us rescue this damsel from such distress!"

Pushing past the false damsel, Sir Lancelot spurred his horse and rode straight toward them at a gallop. With one great blow of his lance, he unhorsed the first man in his way, then went on to another, and another. But now the others closed in on him, and he cast his lance aside and countered their blows with his sword.

The treacherous damsel, watching the fight, smiled with scornful pleasure, for she thought no man could hope to escape a group of more than ten. She did not know the strength and skill of the man she had tried to betray. Lancelot swept through the crowd like the wind of a storm, so that they hardly knew what had hit them. And, when the fighting was over, ten or twelve knights lay stunned on the ground, while Lancelot rode off unharmed. He did not glance back at the damsel who had acted so shamefully toward him, but went on as fast as his horse could go, regretting that so much time had been lost.

The late afternoon shadows already lay on the land when at last the knight saw he was nearing the sword-bridge. There at the very end of the land he saw the castle rise before him, surrounded by dark water. The restless waves beat against the shore, making an angry, pounding noise. Stretching over that churning water — so deep, it appeared to be bottomless — Lancelot saw the sword-bridge, and it was just as bad as he had been told. It was exactly like a well-sharpened sword, but longer than several lances in length. One end was fixed on the shore, in the trunk of a great tree, and the other was driven into the stone of an arched doorway in the side of the castle.

It was not a bridge any man would wish to cross — if he could have his choice. But Lancelot's choice had long been made. Tethering his horse to the tree, he prepared to attempt the crossing. First he removed the gauntlets and greaves from his hands and feet. He knew that this would mean he was likely to be cut to shreds, but he had little fear of wounds, and knew that any such covering would make it all the more difficult for him to keep a firm grasp on the treacherous blade; for, if he should fall into the water, then there would be no escape.

Thus, in terrible agony, he started across the bridge. Blood poured in streams from his hands and his feet before he was halfway across.

6. King Bademagus

From a window above in the castle, the king and his son watched Sir Lancelot cross the sword-bridge. Malagant was almost beside himself with rage; he had not thought that any man would ever manage to make that crossing. It had cost Lancelot the utmost pain, but he had indeed crossed. Now he rested at the end of the bridge, wiping the blood from his gaping wounds.

King Bademagus turned to his son, saying, "We have just seen the most wonderful deed that has ever been done in the memory of men. My heart goes out to that brave knight who has come to our threshold at such terrible cost to himself. I urge you to make your peace with him; if he comes in search of Queen Guinevere — and I am sure that he does — give her over into his hands, without any further ado. It will do you no good to oppose him. Clearly, he is a man unlike any other, and deserving of our respect."

"Do you take me for a weakling," Malagant replied, "that you think I would give up the queen without a struggle? Say, rather, that I should rejoice that yon fool has put himself in my power."

"What power is that?" said Bademagus. "Open your eyes to the truth, my son. You now have little choice but to grant him that which he seeks. For my part, I swear that he shall meet no hostility here from anyone but yourself. I shall see that he does not lack arms if you insist on fighting him. It will be the worse for you if you do not heed my advice, for if he wins your prisoner from you in fair battle, you will be the more shamed, and your other prisoners will all have to be freed at once."

"I defy him," said Malagant. "He will not defeat me so easily."

The king saw that it was useless to argue with his son. "Well, then," he said, "you will do as you please, but I assure you that I will do all I can to see he is treated fairly. I warn you, I am on his side."

He left the room and went with all speed to the entryway, where he found Lancelot tending his wounds. "Sir," Bademagus said, "I am greatly amazed to see you come here thus. You are welcome, with all my heart; I honor you for doing what no other man would dare. I am an old man, as you can see, and have handed over the cares of governing the land to my son. Yet I am still king, and no one will harm you while you are under my protection. I think it very likely that you have come in search of Queen Guinevere."

Lancelot said that this was so. The king spoke again: "Be assured that she is safe, and so she shall remain, for I have seen to that. But I fear that he who brought her here will never agree to give her up without a fight, and you are sorely wounded, and exhausted from your efforts. It is clear that you must rest and be healed before you are fit again. But I shall see that you have the best of care. Come now, sir knight, let me bring you to a chamber fit for so noble a knight."

"I thank you, sire," said Sir Lancelot, "but I am not concerned by my wounds. Take me to your son, I pray; I will not deny him a fight, if that is what he wants."

"Friend," said the king, "you had much better wait until your wounds have had time to heal. I cannot bear to see you put yourself in danger again when you are so much weakened; wait, I beg you, a week or two, at the very least."

Sir Lancelot replied, "Gladly would I go into battle at once, for the sake of my queen; but since you so strongly urge it, I will agree to a delay — but not beyond tomorrow. On no account whatsoever would I wish to linger longer than that."

Reluctantly the king agreed that all should be as he wished. He called his servants to make ready a lodging worthy of his guest, and bid them make haste to do all they could to make him comfortable.

Returning to his son, he said, "Good son, do not fight this valiant man! Pale and weak as he now is, he is more than a match for you. He pays no heed at all to pain, nor fears further suffering. If he had done as I advised, he would have waited to face you in battle when his wounds were healed and his strength regained. But he will not hear of such a delay, and insists he will fight you for the queen tomorrow morning at the latest."

"So much the better," said Malagant. "I am ready whenever he is."

King Bademagus cast a stern glance at his son. "I see," he said, "that it is no use at all to appeal to your honor and pity, for you seem to have neither. May God preserve you from your own headlong folly!"

He sent for a good, strong horse and the best arms in the castle, and had them presented to Sir Lancelot. The most skillful surgeon in the land was called to the knight's bedside, to dress his wounds and bind them carefully. If there had been anything else he could do, the king would have done it, for his noble mind grieved for the brave man.

But while his father was so engaged, Malagant climbed up the stairs of the tower to the room where Guinevere sat with her ladies. The queen was surrounded by every comfort, and guarded by many stern men: not so much in fear that she might escape — that was hardly possible! — but in concern for her safety. King Bademagus had reason not to trust his son, and so he had decreed that if the queen were to be held in his castle, she must have personal bodyguards who would see that she came to no harm. So it happened that even Malagant, much to his annoyance, could not enter the queen's rooms without her express permission, nor speak to her without a watchful guard standing by.

Time hung heavy on the ladies' hands, there in the tower room, for they had little to do. They would have tended their wounded knights, who lay in a nearby room, but the king had seen that they were so well attended there was not much the ladies could do. They took little pleasure in needlework, for they were far from the halls they would have cared to adorn. Neither had they the heart for dancing and singing, captives as they were. Mostly they sat in dull silence, dreaming of home, and listening, from time to time, as one of their number remembered a tale of Camelot, and told it to the rest.

Therefore, they were not unhappy when the guard told them Malagant was there, and wished to speak to the queen. Guinevere herself agreed that even such a visitor, for whom they had little love, might serve as a welcome diversion to while away an hour. And so Malagant was admitted, and the queen received him courteously enough.

46

"Madame," said Sir Malagant, "I hardly know how to tell you the terrible news I bring."

A shudder ran around the room. What more could happen now? The ladies drew close around Guinevere, who remained perfectly calm, and asked what news he brought.

"I very much fear," said Malagant, "that word of your coming hither has reached the worst sort of evildoer. There has been a rumor in the land that a desperate criminal has come over the border, and that he has been seen making his way to this castle. My people have no doubt that he intends to lay his hands on you, my lady, in hope of collecting a huge ransom from your lord King Arthur. Despite all our efforts to stop this villain, I fear that he has now succeeded so well that he is here in this castle.

"He has deluded the king my father into granting him protection, and demands, in his impudence, that I fight him in the morning. If he should win, he would demand that I hand over your person; but, of course, that is unthinkable. I hate to think what might happen to you in the hands of such a churl."

The ladies were much agitated, but Guinevere cast her eyes down and wondered what to think. She certainly did not trust Sir Malagant. Even if he had told her the truth, would one captor be worse than another?

At length, she simply said, "Sir, I should much like to see the man who has actually broken into this castle, for I marvel how it could be done."

"You shall see him soon enough, unless your good fortune preserves you," Sir Malagant replied. "I should hardly think that your majesty would care to converse with a common fellow who has been held up to shame in a cart."

To this the queen would make no reply, so that Malagant could not help but see that she considered the interview over. He bowed, somewhat ungraciously, and left her, as the ladies fluttered around the room, all talking at once. "What is to become of us now?" one wailed, and soon they would all have burst into tears if the queen had not said quietly, "Be still, my friends, and we shall see if the news is bad or good. Surely it was no common man who has found us in this place."

"But a criminal — !" sobbed a young maiden.

"If he is a villain, indeed," said the queen, "I fancy that King Bademagus will see that we come to no harm. But for now we must be patient. We know not what the morrow may bring."

7. Guinevere Found

*T*he place appointed for the battle between Sir Lancelot and Sir Malagant was the castle square. Early the next morning, the people of the castle began to gather there. Those who were captives in the land prayed for the victory of the strange knight, for they had heard that he fought to deliver them all. When the two knights were led in fully armed, there was much jostling in the crowd, for all were anxious to have a good view.

Malagant was a tall and imposing man, and he was an impressive figure in his armor. Still, the crowd favored Sir Lancelot; even the natives of the land had to admit that they had never seen a more noble-looking knight. But, stern and erect as he looked, in truth he was far from commanding his full strength that morning. If ever Sir Malagant had a chance to defeat Sir Lancelot, this would be the day.

Both knights were now in their places, with their lances ready. Before the signal sounded, the king came onto the field, and tried once more to make peace between them; but Malagant stubbornly refused to be persuaded. The king then moved to his seat, and the knights charged at each other with such force that both lances broke. The horses met head on, and there was such a crash that all their trappings broke apart — reins, girth, and saddle straps went in all directions, and the two riders fell to the ground.

Losing no time, they sprang to their feet, drew their swords, and rushed at each other without a word, fighting as fiercely as two wild boars. The square rang with the sound of steel striking on steel, as sparks flew from their helmets. Their swords flashed

in the sunlight, as one blow countered the next so swiftly that no one could have kept count. For a while the match seemed so even that neither appeared to have the advantage.

But soon those who hoped for the strange knight's triumph began to feel some dismay, for his blows seemed to be growing weaker, and Sir Malagant pressed him hard. This was, of course, what Malagant had expected, for he knew that Lancelot must be weakened by the wounds on his hands and feet. Nonetheless, Lancelot stood his ground.

At last the time came when Malagant began to tire, and his blows faltered a bit. Lancelot mustered his strength and will and rushed so upon Malagant that he seemed to be dealing blows from all directions at once; the battle had turned in his favor. With no thought for the pain of his wounds, Sir Lancelot struck again and again, until at last King Bademagus feared for his son's life.

Bademagus jumped up from his seat. "Halt! Enough!" he called, as he sent his men down to the field to separate the two knights. Sir Lancelot put up his sword at once, but Malagant, furious that the fight had had to be stopped for his sake, lunged against his foe and struck him as hard as he could. "What!" cried the king. "Would you strike a man who withholds his blows from you? For shame, my son! There is no doubt at all that he has defeated you."

Still Malagant would not have held back, but the king's men restrained him by force. Still he insisted he was not defeated, saying, "Stand aside and let us fight! I shall defeat him yet!" But the king would by no means allow the fight to resume.

54

"I will not stand by and see you go to your death through your own pride and folly," said King Bademagus. "Whether you will or no, you must now make terms, and agree at the very least to a truce for the time being."

Sir Malagant did not like this at all, but as his father allowed him no choice, he had, in the end, to agree; but he insisted on setting the terms of the truce. The terms that he asked were these: that Queen Guinevere would be surrendered to Sir Lancelot, and allowed to return to Camelot, providing that Lancelot agreed to fight him again within a year of such time as he should ask it, at Arthur's court, in the presence of the knights of the Round Table. If Lancelot should lose the battle, or if he should fail to appear, the queen would be returned to Malagant, to remain his prisoner forever more, and no man would lift a hand to prevent this.

Sir Lancelot accepted these terms readily enough, though to many it seemed wonderful that Malagant was willing to risk a second fight. It was hardly likely that Lancelot would be as much weakened a year hence as he had been that day, yet even so he had been too much for Malagant.

Now it remained for the queen to give her consent to the terms. King Bademagus went to her himself, and explained the agreement to her. He was much astonished when he saw that she hesitated. "But who," she asked, "is this knight to whom I should be surrendered? Do you not know his name?"

Bademagus replied, "I have not asked him his name, nor has he told it to me. But I know that he is as brave a knight as I have ever seen."

"Many a wicked and desperate man is brave enough," said the queen. "But I have heard that the man who came hither in search of me is no true knight, but an outcast, a criminal."

"That I do not believe, dear lady," said the king. "I shall bring him to you, and you shall judge for yourself."

He left her hurriedly, and soon returned with Sir Lancelot, who dropped to his knee before his queen. Then Guinevere's heart was filled with joy: she knew that good knight well.

Queen Guinevere held out her hand and bade Sir Lancelot rise, saying, "Never were you more welcome, sir. Are you, then, the Knight of the Cart, of whose coming we were told?"

And when Lancelot said that this was so, she turned to her

ladies and said, "Never should we have believed for a moment the lies of Sir Malagant! He who has come to rescue us is no evildoer, but the best knight in the world. Behold, it is Sir Lancelot!"

Soon the queen took Lancelot to the room where her wounded knights were lying, and they rejoiced greatly to see him. Lancelot wept with pity to see their wounds, never remembering his own. When he had told them of his perilous journey, and how Malagant had tried again and again to stop him, by fair means and foul, they were all greatly indignant and yearned for revenge. A coward who would set archers at a good man's horse, and beset his way with false spies to deceive him, did not deserve to live, they murmured.

For the time, though, they knew they must keep the peace. They hoped to see Sir Lancelot defeat him soundly yet, though some were very doubtful that Malagant would, in the end, dare to demand a second fight.

If there was great rejoicing in the queen's tower rooms, there was just as much joy throughout the land, for now that the queen was to be released, all other prisoners were also free to go wherever they wished. Many hearts were merry in the land of Gorre that night; laughter was heard in places where yesterday there had been nothing but sighs. But as for Sir Lancelot himself, his mind was sorely troubled. He had had no word of his dear comrade, Sir Gawain, since the two had parted where the two roads branched.

And so, when the next morning came, Sir Lancelot went to King Bademagus. "Sire," he said, "I must ask your leave to go and search for Sir Gawain, the noble knight who shared my quest with me. We parted at the border of your land, I to take the road to the sword-bridge, and he to follow that which leads to the water-bridge. I cannot rest easy in my mind until I know what has become of him."

The king granted his permission, and it was arranged that for a little while longer Guinevere would remain in the castle, where she would be safe enough, until such time as Sir Lancelot returned with Sir Gawain to escort her back to Camelot.

Lancelot made ready to go, impatient to seek his friend. The king's chief boatman was summoned to carry him over the water. Several noble lords of the castle also gathered to escort the knight over the water, although he declined their offer to ride with him in search of Sir Gawain.

And so Lancelot set out from the castle — and you may be sure that the journey back to the shore was a great deal more pleasant than the trip over had been.

8. Lancelot Lost

*S*ir Lancelot's goal on the shore was the water-bridge, of course, since it was on the route that led there that he must seek for Sir Gawain, or hope to hear some word of him. But since he had left his horse tethered to the tree at the end of the sword-bridge, he directed the boatman to land him there; from that spot, he would find his way to the landing by the water-bridge.

Coming ashore by the great tree, he found his horse right where he had left him. A dwarf, leading a second horse, also waited under the tree. He bowed to Sir Lancelot. "Sir," the dwarf said, "I bring you greetings from my lord Sir Gawain. He is in great need of your help. If you will come with me, I will take you to him. But hasten — there is no time to be lost!"

Lancelot mounted his horse at once, asking no questions in his haste to come to Gawain's aid. Forgetting even to turn back to say farewell to the knights who had escorted him, he rode off after the dwarf, who led the way.

The boatman turned back to return to the castle. But as he did so, one of the knights in the boat cried out in surprise, saying, "Look, there by the water-bridge! Surely someone is trying to make the crossing!"

Quickly the boat turned, and they made for the water-bridge with all possible speed. When they reached it they found Sir Gawain, who at that very moment had slipped and fallen on the narrow, treacherous span. He sank from their sight in the water, then rose for a moment before he sank again. The king's men rushed with poles and hooks and tried their best to raise him from the water, but it was very difficult, for Gawain was much weighed down by his heavy armor. Finally they succeeded in getting him up into the boat, but they did not think that he was alive. They set to work to do all they could to get the water out of his body, until at long last Gawain opened his eyes and managed to speak a few words. Weakly, he asked for news of the queen.

All those present rejoiced that he would live, and assured him that the queen was perfectly safe, and that they would take him to her at once. "Has no one come to seek her, to bring her out of this land?" Gawain asked.

"Yes, indeed," was the answer. And when Gawain asked them who had come, they told him how Sir Lancelot had crossed the sword-bridge and succeeded in his quest, adding, "We have just now put him on shore, where he met a dwarf who said he was sent by you, my lord — if you are, as we think, Sir Gawain."

Greatly alarmed, Gawain said, "But I sent no dwarf to him! I fear he has met with some treachery." And he wished to go right back and set out in search of Sir Lancelot. But the others urged him strongly to come to the castle first. There he would see his queen, and reassure her that he was alive and well. Then they would ask the king to have the land searched for Lancelot, for all were of the opinion that Malagant must be to blame for any treachery that might be afoot.

When he had heard the whole story, Gawain was inclined to agree, and went with them to the castle. There Queen Guinevere received him with joy, until she heard how Lancelot had, it seemed, been tricked away, and had gone no man knew whither. Then her joy was mixed with such fear and grief that she did not know whether to be merry for Gawain's sake or to weep for Lancelot.

Likewise, King Bademagus was torn between gladness at the coming of Sir Gawain and distress for the missing Lancelot. He called his son to him at once, and demanded with great sternness what had befallen Sir Lancelot. Malagant, however, denied that he had any knowledge of Lancelot's whereabouts. The king did not believe this, but there was little he could do in the face of Malagant's continued denials, except to send out messengers, and to proclaim throughout the land that he, King Bademagus, would richly reward anyone who helped to find the knight.

His men-at-arms rode far and wide, but when they returned to the castle after several days' search, they had no news at all to report. Lancelot had disappeared, and nowhere was there to be found any trace of him. Gloom lay over the castle, for everyone, native and stranger, mourned for the brave knight whose feats had impressed them all.

At last it was decided that there was nothing left to do but start back to King Arthur's court, for Guinevere's knights were now quite recovered from their wounds, and all the former captives longed to return to their homes. Then, just as the men were arming and the ladies preparing to ride, a messenger suddenly appeared, bearing a letter for the queen. It was read before all the company, and this is what it said: that Lancelot sent greetings to his queen and also to King Bademagus; that he thanked the king for the honor and kindness he had shown him, and that he would be glad to do him service if it ever should be in his power; that he had now returned to Arthur's court, where all awaited the queen; he bid her come, with Sir Gawain, and join him there.

When this letter had been read, everyone thanked God that Sir Lancelot was safe, and all the castle rang with gladness. The king ordered a great feast in honor of these welcome tidings, and the messenger who had brought the letter was treated with every honor. Thus it was not until morning that the group again assembled to start on the trip home. The king himself rode out with them, escorting them to the border of his land, where he took his leave of Queen Guinevere.

In gratitude for his kindness, the queen embraced Bademagus and kissed him on both cheeks, swearing that she and her
lord would look for a chance to repay his favor to her. For his
part, Sir Gawain vowed that he would come at once if ever the
good king had need of him, and so did all the rest of the queen's
men, before they went on their way.

The next day there was joy indeed in Camelot, when word
reached the king that Queen Guinevere and Sir Gawain were
riding into the court. Arthur rode out to meet them, with a great
throng of knights and ladies.

Noblemen, servants, and townsmen alike ran to greet them,
crying, "Welcome to Sir Gawain, who has rescued our queen and
delivered our captive people!"

But when he could make himself heard, Sir Gawain
answered them, "Pray do not make me ashamed; I do not

66

deserve your praise. I could not reach the queen in time, so long was I held up on my way. It is Sir Lancelot who has done this great deed, and won all honor for himself."

"But where, then, is Sir Lancelot?" King Arthur inquired. "I do not see him here."

"Is he not with you?" asked Gawain. "Surely he must be here at court, for we had word from him that he awaited us here."

"Nay," answered the king, "he has not been seen here, or anywhere in this land, since the day the queen was taken. Nor have we heard from him."

Then it became quite clear that the letter must have been forged. They had been sadly deceived. The joyous homecoming was now all but spoiled, as laments for Sir Lancelot were heard on all sides, and the queen wept bitterly.

9. Lancelot in Captivity

*T*he treacherous Sir Malagant had, as everyone suspected, arranged for Sir Lancelot to be tricked and trapped into imprisonment. Malagant knew well that his enemy was safely locked up where no one was likely to find him, and where, no matter how strong he was, he could not possibly break loose.

Now he proceeded to Camelot, and appeared before King Arthur. He spoke up boldly before the court: "King, I have come to serve notice of my desire to fight a battle, according to the terms which were laid down with Sir Lancelot when I agreed to release the queen. But I do not see Sir Lancelot among those here at your court. If he is here, let him step forth and swear to fulfill his vow to meet me in battle. I demand that he be here, prepared to defend your right to retain the queen, on this day one year hence."

"Friend," said King Arthur, "I fear I cannot answer for Sir Lancelot. He is not here, nor do we know where he is."

Malagant replied, "He has vowed to meet me here. I hereby challenge him to keep his promise and fight me a year from today."

Sir Gawain turned to the king and said, "Sire, we know not what has become of Lancelot, nor whether he will be here when this day comes. If he should not appear, grant me the battle: I will gladly fight for him, and for my lady the queen."

"Nay," said Sir Malagant, "that was not our agreement. Sir Lancelot must fight for himself, or, if he does not appear, the battle is forfeited, and you must give me Queen Guinevere."

The queen was greatly distressed, but she agreed that such had been the terms. So, too, did all those there who had been in captivity with her.

"In that case, sire," said Gawain, "let me go in search of Sir Lancelot. I know well that he would never fail to keep his promise in such a case, unless he were sick, dead, or in prison."

Malagant reminded him that a search had already been made throughout the land of Gorre, to no avail. "Seek for him if you wish," he added, "wherever you think he may be, but I swear, for my part, that if he is not here on the appointed day, I shall demand my right to have the queen given to me, to keep as my prisoner forever more. Your court will be dishonored before all the world if you fail to keep that agreement."

With that, he left King Arthur's court, and rode back to his own land. He was very pleased with himself. He went at once to his father, King Bademagus, who held high feast that day, for it was the good king's birthday. All the noblemen of the land were gathered in the king's court when Sir Malagant came into the hall before his father, and said, "Father, rejoice with me. I have been to King Arthur's court and found that all there fear me. Even Sir Lancelot has fled, and is in hiding, rather than face me in battle again. Is not any knight to be held great when his arms are feared at Arthur's court?"

"Son," said King Bademagus, "I am amazed at your foolishness. It is not possible that Sir Lancelot should hide in fear of you. I am sure that he must be either dead or in prison, though I should greatly grieve to hear of that brave knight's death. You are no son of mine if you persist in your folly, or in declaring the battle forfeited if he should not appear. Please God, it may not come to that!"

Malagant, white with fury, turned and left the room. Bademagus said no more, but sat bowed with shame for his son. He

hardly noticed Malagant's parting curse. But there was a lady there who had listened carefully to every word which had been spoken. This lady was the daughter of Bademagus, and sister of Malagant.

She was a wise and virtuous maiden, and she had her own good reasons for being concerned for Sir Lancelot. It seemed perfectly clear to her that he must have been taken prisoner, since there had been no news of him from the moment when he had vanished in the company of the dwarf. It was equally clear to her that this must be the work of her brother, Sir Malagant. To herself she vowed she would never rest until she had found Sir Lancelot. She rose from her chair at the feast so quietly that no one realized she had gone.

Quickly, she went to the stable and saddled a swift mule — all the servants were elsewhere, feasting, and no one was there to see as she rode silently away. She had no idea which way she should go. Since one way was as likely as any other, it seemed best for her to take the first road she found and ride along at random, searching every possible hiding place — manor, cottage, cave, or shed — as best she could. And thus she rode on for many a day, quite alone, never stopping long in any place. But nowhere did she find any clue to lead her to Lancelot. So she had ridden on for many a long month, over hills and dales and in many strange lands, and had learned nothing more than what she had known before — which was nothing at all. Then one day, when she was crossing a field, sad and dejected in mood, she saw a distant tower on a neck of the land by the edge of the sea. It stood alone in the midst of a desolate land, where there was no tree or dwelling to be seen for many a mile, nor any other sign of life about. As she fixed her eye on this tower, hope began to rise in her heart again: this was just such a barren and remote spot as Sir Malagant might have chosen to hide away a prisoner.

She drew near to the tower, dismounted, and walked around it. The tower was strong and high, with thick stone walls. There did not seem to be any doorway in it, although she noted a place where the uneven masonry suggested that a door had once been

there, and was now walled up. Nor did she see any windows, except for one small hole, high up in the tower.

The steep, sheer wall of the tower rose to this small opening without any ladder or steps. There seemed, finally, to be no way at all by which she could enter the tower. Yet, the more she saw of this grim place, the more she thought it likely that Sir Lancelot was imprisoned there. She sat down on the ground and pondered what she ought to do next; perhaps she should go for help, to force a way into the tower. But just then she heard a voice which seemed to come from the window above. It was clearly a prisoner, bemoaning his unhappy lot — but it did not sound at all like Sir Lancelot, for the voice was thin and weak.

"Alas," said the voice, in a low, hoarse tone, "why does my

life drag on so long? — Ah, my old friend Gawain, why have you deserted me here? If you had been thus made captive, I would surely have found you ere now. But the weary months go on, and still you do not come to my aid. — May God's curse fall on the vile man who has brought me to such a state! Malagant, surely you must be the very worst man alive."

"Sir Lancelot!" called the princess. "Is it your voice I hear?" But the man inside the tower did not hear her words. Again she called, as loudly as she could, and again, until the knight finally heard her voice calling his name; but he did not know who it might be. Greatly astonished, he looked about him to see where the voice came from. There was certainly no one in his prison with him. "Alas," he said, "can it be I am losing my mind?

Surely I have lived too long when I hear voices where no man is present!"

Trying to raise her voice still louder, the princess called his name beneath the window again. Slowly, with feeble steps, he made his way to the window, and looked down, until he saw a lady standing there. He did not recognize her, and was greatly astonished, wondering who she might be.

"Ah, Lancelot," cried the princess, "thank God I have found you at last! I am she whose boon you granted at the ford. When you spared the life of my knight there, I vowed that I would return the favor whenever it lay in my power. Now I can fulfill my vow by freeing you from your prison."

"Sweet lady," said Sir Lancelot, "if you can do that, I will be in your debt forever. Ask for anything I may have, and it shall be yours at once."

"Have no fear," said the princess; "you shall be released this very day. I shall go at once to find a tool with which you can enlarge that opening so that you may pass through easily. And we must also have some rope."

"There is rope enough right here," answered Lancelot. "My jailors left it here, for me to use to pull up the scanty food they give me — vile barley bread and water! They know I cannot use it to escape, for, though thin and weakened, I am still not small enough to creep through this hole in the wall."

"Be patient a little while yet," said the princess. "I shall soon have you out of there. Then I shall take you to my manor, where you will have food enough, and can rest while you gain back your strength. Now I shall go in search of a pick: I trust I shall not be long."

10. The Knight on the
White Horse

*O*n the appointed day, Sir Malagant appeared at King Arthur's court and demanded to know whether Lancelot were ready to do battle. But Sir Lancelot was not there, nor did anyone know what had become of him. Sir Malagant thought he knew where Lancelot was, of course, but he pretended to be much surprised not to find him there.

"For my part, I kept the agreement, sire," said Malagant to the king. "Now it is up to you to see that justice is done, since Sir Lancelot has failed to keep his promise. I declare the battle forfeited: hand over Queen Guinevere, or be proved a false breaker of treaties!"

King Arthur could only ask Sir Malagant to wait until such time as it might be found what had befallen Sir Lancelot, but Malagant angrily refused. "I gave a year's notice, my lord king," he said, "and that was time enough."

Then Sir Gawain repeated his offer to fight on behalf of Sir Lancelot, but this was also refused with scorn. Thus there seemed no choice but for the queen to make ready to ride away into hopeless captivity. Everyone there was oppressed with sorrow, and there was not a dry eye in the court — except for those of the treacherous Malagant, whose eyes glittered with triumph, rather than tears, as he exulted at the thought that he had rendered the greatest court in the world helpless to defy him.

Just as he was about to lead off the weeping queen, a great cry was heard without, and many people appeared to be running that way. Everyone turned to see what the uproar might be. There they saw, riding toward them at a great speed, a splendid knight, his shining armor gleaming in the sun, mounted upon a white horse.

It was Sir Lancelot, returned at last, once more mounted on his own horse, who was fully recovered, as was his master. "Hold, Sir Malagant!" called Lancelot, in a voice like thunder. "Today you shall have what you deserve, but it is not to be Queen Guinevere."

Sir Malagant was struck dumb with amazement, and almost fainted for fear. "Ah, what a fool I was," he thought, "to have failed to go, before I came hither, to see that Sir Lancelot was safely confined in my tower! How can he possibly have escaped? Somebody must have betrayed me, alas! Well, it must be faced now; perhaps he is still so weakened by his diet of bread and water that I may triumph yet."

Now all proceeded to the field where preparations had been made for the battle to be held. The king and queen and all the knights and ladies of the court came to watch, with new hope in their hearts. When the king had given his command that the crowd draw back and make room, Lancelot aimed his spear at Sir Malagant, shouting, "Stand and defend yourself, villain! This time you shall not be spared!"

The horses galloped and charged to the middle of the field. As they met, Lancelot's spear took Malagant right off his horse. Quickly Sir Lancelot jumped down from his steed, his shield on his shoulder and his sword in his right hand, and the two enemies lashed out at each other with the utmost fury. But Sir Malagant was not able to keep up with his foe this time, and it was not very long before Sir Lancelot hit him such a stroke on his helmet that he fell dazed to the ground.

"I cry your mercy," Malagant gasped. "Lancelot, I yield to

you — I am utterly overcome. I beg that you spare my life!"

But Sir Lancelot was in no mood to be merciful to the traitor who had caused him — and all the rest of Arthur's people — such great suffering. "Rise up, for shame," he said. "I bid you fight it out with me to the end."

82

"On no account," said Sir Malagant; "I shall never rise until you grant me my life as a defeated prisoner."

"In that case," said Sir Lancelot, "I shall make you an offer. I will put aside my helmet and shield and let my left arm be bound behind my back, and thus do battle with you."

Sir Malagant rose up at once, saying, "My lord King Arthur, you have heard what he has said. Let him be so bound, before we fight again."

"Will you abide by that?" asked King Arthur of Lancelot.

"Indeed, sire," said Sir Lancelot; "I have said it, and I will not go back on my word."

Then the squires attending the knights took off Sir Lancelot's helmet and shield, and bound his left hand behind his back. There was a great stir among those who watched, for many a knight and lady were greatly astounded that Sir Lancelot would put himself in such danger.

Sir Malagant now rushed at him, wielding his sword with all his might. But Sir Lancelot moved with such speed and skill that none of Malagant's blows could touch him. Again and again he dealt Sir Malagant such great blows that at last Malagant fell to the earth with a crash. But this time he did not rise again.

And so the battle was over. There was nothing to do but carry Sir Malagant, now so sorely wounded that it was clear he would not recover, off from the field on his shield. No one there had any cause to be very sorry for that! The king and all the others could hardly express their delight as they rushed to disarm Sir Lancelot, and lead him in triumph to the hall, where he sat in the place of honor, as all the bells of Camelot rang out in joy.

Far away in the land of Gorre, even King Bademagus could not mourn very much for the loss of such a son. For when spring had come again to Gorre, as it had to Camelot, Bademagus had given a great wedding feast for his daughter the princess, who was as lovely as she was wise; now he hoped he would soon have a grandson to rule over his land after him. And when the day came that a son was born to the princess, there was great rejoicing throughout the land.

A messenger was sent to Arthur's court, to remind the queen and her men of the promises they had made to come to King Bademagus whenever he needed them. Now he sent word that he needed them — to come to the christening party, and do honor to his grandson.

So the folk of Camelot rode again to the castle of Gorre, this time in great strength and magnificence, and with much merriment, and Sir Lancelot was godfather to the son of the princess who had once rescued him from his prison.

About the Illustrator

John Gretzer has spent much of his life in the Midwest. He was born in Council Bluffs, Iowa, attended the University of Omaha, and studied at the Kansas City Art Institute for a year under Thomas Hart Benton.

Mr. Gretzer has been active in the production of animated movies and in department-store advertising. He was at one time art director for a publishing firm and now undertakes free-lance assignments involving advertising and editorial art. He is the illustrator of several books for children.

Mr. Gretzer and his family live in Perkasie, Pennsylvania.

About the Author

As a medieval scholar, Constance Hieatt has especially enjoyed retelling Arthurian legends for young readers. THE KNIGHT OF THE CART is a companion volume to her earlier books, *Sir Gawain and the Green Knight* and *The Knight of the Lion*. Mrs. Hieatt is a specialist in Old and Middle English, and the author of several texts, translations, and scholarly commentaries. She has taught at Queensborough Community College and St. John's University in New York, and is now at the University of Western Ontario in London, Ontario.

Mrs. Hieatt was born in Boston, Massachusetts, and attended Smith College. She received her A.B. and A.M. degrees from Hunter College, and her Ph.D. from Yale University. She and her husband, who is also a professor of English, spend much of their time in England, where their home is part of a remodeled manor house in a village near Oxford.